The Witch of Monopoly Manor

"I feel like a duchess!" whooped the witch as she put on a diamond tiara. Having decided that her own house was not suitably grand, the witch had moved into Monopoly Manor and started living the high life.

She gave a splendid house-warming party, which ended in chaos, and opened a Safari Park on the grounds with wild animals imported from Africa. Needless to say, Lady Fox-Custard was horrified at having the witch as her new neighbour and did her best to get rid of her. And, as usual, Simon found that the witch was getting him into some dreadful scrapes . . .

The Witch of Monopoly Manor

MARGARET STUART BARRY

Illustrated by Linda Birch

YOUNG LIONS

First published in Great Britain 1980
by William Collins Sons & Co. Ltd
First published in Young Lions 1981
Seventh impression March 1990

Young Lions is an imprint of
the Children's Division, part of
the Collins Publishing Group,
8 Grafton Street, London W1X 3LA

Printed and bound in Great Britain by
William Collins Sons & Co. Ltd, Glasgow

Contents

To Eve, Francoise,
Zoe and Paul

Christmas Eve

It was Christmas Eve and Simon was out doing his last-minute shopping. He'd bought most of his presents but he still could not think what to give his mother.

It was snowing, and the noise of the traffic was muffled. Simon loved it. The snow made the High Street seem different, as if it belonged to a time long past. The lighted shops looked cosier and less familiar. And the butcher, who was usually a bit short-tempered, had a sprig of holly in his hat and was beaming at the customers from behind a row of enormous turkeys.

"Oh, super!" said Simon, sludging along excitedly.

An old man was singing carols, his cap on the ground filling with snow. Simon put a penny in it, and the old man said, "Thank you lad. Merry Christmas!"

Farther down the road crouched an old woman, also singing. Her hat stuck in the snow easily as it was long and very pointed.

"Oh no," groaned Simon, "I can't give anything to *her*. I'll have no money left."

He turned his head and pretended to stare at a boy who was pulling a Christmas tree along on a sledge.

"Meaney!" shrieked the old woman.

Simon recognized that voice immediately: it sounded like a mixture of a lorry load of gravel being unloaded and a factory siren.

"The *witch*!" he cried.

"Ha ha," laughed the witch. "Yes, it's me! It's *me*!"

"What are you doing singing on the pavement?"

"Finding out who is the meanest boy in town and you are!" cackled the witch.

People were beginning to stare, so Simon dragged the witch into the chemist's and told her to be a bit quieter and help him choose a present for his mother. The witch didn't help at all, but fooled around so much she was thrown out by the manager, and Simon had to choose some soap in a hurry and follow her.

"Have you got a Christmas tree yet?" he panted, running and skidding after the witch.

The year before, the witch, who didn't believe in going to any unnecessary expense, had pulled up an oak sapling from her front garden and used that for a Christmas tree.

"Done better than last year," she chuckled. "Just wait till you see."

When they reached the witch's house, Simon saw a privet hedge running the full length of the witch's sitting room. The roots were kept moist in a collection of biscuit tins. It was hung all along with black stockings, waiting to be filled. There were one or two glass balls and wisps of tinsel on it, but for the most part the witch had decorated it herself. In the middle of the hedge was the orange top of a Belisha beacon, (the wind had blown it clean off, the witch explained) and a candle was burning inside it. This bothered Simon a little as the firemen were all out on strike and the candle looked dangerous. Brown paper parcels tied up with string hung from the leaves and, perched on the branches within, were birds of every different sort. There was even a duck, nesting in one of the biscuit tins.

"Stuffed of course," explained the witch.

But George, the witch's cat, who was permanently ravenous on account of the witch's permanently forgetting to feed him, was sniffing hungrily at the birds. Suddenly, he attacked a sparrow which happened to be looking the wrong way and was disgusted to find out it was full of cotton wool. George was sneezing feathers and cotton wool everywhere.

"Oh, I suffer with this greedy cat!" complained the witch. "Wretched, wretched animal!" She hurled a tin of Pussy's Delight and a tin opener at it and dragged Simon excitedly over to the mantlepiece to show him her Christmas cards. She had received cards from all her relations: Hattie

The Howl, Winnie from Wapping, Awful Aggie, and others too numerous to mention.

Simon was delighted to be sitting in the witch's house again. She was his best friend and never behaved the way other people did. He wished his mother and his school friends believed in her, but they didn't. At the thought of his mother, busy at home, he said that he must be going.

"I really must go," he said.

"You can't," said the witch. "Have a beetle sandwich."

"But my mother'll be wanting to get me ready for bed."

"D'you have to get *ready* for bed?" asked the witch, puzzled. "I just take my hat off. I'll make you a boring old banana sandwich and then you can ring your mother and tell her you'll be a bit late home."

Simon felt helpless. The witch had a habit of getting her own way. On the other hand, it was snowing fast outside and drifting up high against the window panes, whereas the witch's fire was burning red and hotly. He rang his mother.

George prowled across the rug and sniffed up the chimney.

"What's he doing?" asked Simon.

"Oh, the fool animal's waiting for Father Christmas to come down!" snorted the witch.

"Someone's stuffed the poor creature's head full of rubbish. Last year there was a sooty packet of fish fingers in the hearth and he swears they were left there by this old man in red. Watches too much television he does!"

The witch was very scornful, but secretly she, too, was waiting up to catch Father Christmas. She wanted to see if he really came down chimneys. This is why she had wanted Simon to stay with her, but in spite of the interesting programmes on television Simon began to feel sleepy. The witch kept making him fresh banana sandwiches and dabbing his head with ice cream but still Simon fell asleep. It was just as he finally slumped into a cushion that Father Christmas came rattling down the chimney. He overshot the hot fire and landed in a heap on the rug.

"Good evening," said the witch, pretending like mad not to be surprised and remembering, politely, how hurtful it was not to be believed in.

"I've been ages on your roof," shivered Father Christmas. "I thought that boy would never fall asleep."

"I was trying to keep him *awake*," said the witch.

"Oh no," said Father Christmas. "You obviously don't know a lot about Christmas. I never let children see me."

"Why not?" asked the witch.

Father Christmas plonked down in an armchair and thought. "I don't know," he said at last. "No one has ever asked me that question before so I've never thought about it."

He warmed his toes by the fire and then said, "Does anyone ever ask you to explain your magic spells?"

"Certainly not!" exclaimed the witch, aghast.

"Well it's the same sort of thing with me," said Father Christmas.

"Get on!" squealed the witch. And she rolled round and round the floor, laughing and wheezing and feeling proud of being unusual and having such an important, jolly visitor. Even George felt pleased and showed off by eating a coffee table in two mouthfuls.

"We'd better be getting this boy back to his home," said Father Christmas. "So if you don't mind I'll give my reindeer a rest on your roof and we'll take a taxi."

He hid a leather case for the witch's wand and a packet of cod in parsley sauce under the privet hedge and helped to carry Simon out to a waiting taxi.

Simon's mother was still cooking in the kitchen, as Father Christmas and the witch crept in through the French windows and took Simon up to bed.

"He's got to get ready, or something peculiar like that," whispered the witch.

"Of course," whispered Father Christmas. "Brush his teeth and fetch his pyjamas."

"What a carry on!" giggled the witch.

"Now we must look for a note," whispered Father Christmas.

"What note?" whispered the witch.

"The one saying what he wants for Christmas," whispered Father Christmas back.

"Why are we whispering so much?" whispered the witch.

"*Everyone* whispers on Christmas Eve," whispered Father Christmas.

"Oh!" shrieked the witch, forgetting. "I've found the note. It's in the fireplace!"

Simon had asked for a train set, and just as Father Christmas began to unpack it, they heard Simon's mother coming upstairs.

Father Christmas and the witch dived under the bed, or half under it that is, as they came nose to nose with a platoon full of soldiers bearing fixed bayonets.

"What a daft time to start a war!" snorted the witch, looking the Major General wickedly in the eye.

"They'll do us a lot of mischief with those weapons," grumbled Father Christmas.

"Oh no!" said Simon's mother, who could plainly see nearly all of the couple hiding under the bed. "What a time to come visiting. Simon's asleep."

But she took them downstairs to the kitchen, and gave them a warming glass of sherry and a mince pie. She felt sorry for old-aged pensioners at Christmas time.

Next day, Simon jumped out of bed early and played with his train set, then he went down to breakfast and gave his mother the soap.

She looked pleased and smelt it a lot, but had to say, "Simon, I *do* wish you wouldn't have that old woman friend of yours round so late. And she'd brought a poor old man with her from one of the stores."

"That would have been Father Christmas!" gasped Simon. "Me and the witch were waiting up for him for ages!"

"Yes dear," sighed his mother, not believing a word of it. "Well, they should have been at home in bed. It was far too late for them to be out." And she hurried off to stuff the turkey, leaving Simon to wonder about it all.

The Terrible New Neighbour

Simon and the witch enjoyed the Christmas holiday enormously, but towards the end of it there came a "nothingish" sort of time. The snow had turned into ginger yellow slush, and it wasn't icy enough to slide on, yet it was too chilly to play other games outside.

"I'm fed up!" said the witch.

"Why?" asked Simon.

"I just am," snapped the witch, flapping her black dress around her like an angry bat. "I mean – just look at this silly, little, squashy house I live in, not enough room to swing a cat in it!"

George, the witch's long-suffering cat, skulked off under the sideboard. He was used to the witch's tantrums and had been swung round by the tail more times than he could count, and was not in the mood for aerobatics that day.

"I like it," Simon said, looking round at the cluttered living room. "It's cosy."

"*Cosy!*" boomed the witch. "It's squashy! Do you imagine this is a suitable residence for a witch?"

"I don't think . . ." began Simon.

"I've noticed that!" shrieked the witch, leaping all round the room; over the top of the sofa, under the television, up the curtains, in the most alarming manner. "Where would be a more suitable place for me to live?"

"Maybe in the middle of a dark forest."

"With a toadstool for a chimney I suppose!" scoffed the witch. "You read too many stupid fairy tales. We're going house-hunting tomorrow. Be here early."

Next morning, the witch was waiting on her doorstep. She was dressed up as if prepared for some sort of battle. Her Sunday-best hat was safety-pinned to a shoelace, which in turn was safety-pinned to her collar. Round her neck were wound ten yards of hen's feathers. Her buttons were all correctly popped through the right buttonholes. Over her arm hung the massive shabby handbag she took with her everywhere. It contained everything she prized most: her pension book, her cat George, tomorrow's racing results, and her magic wand, heavily repaired with Elastoplast.

Simon arrived in his anorak and wellingtons.

"Hullo," he said.

"Ready?" said the witch.

They went down the road to the house agents, which is a place where one goes when one is looking for a house to buy. There they found a fat lady in a blonde wig. She had shiny red nails, was sitting behind a swish shiny counter, and was surrounded by a vast amount of shiny photographs of shining houses.

"What were you looking for?" she asked.

"A hutch to keep my shiny rabbits in!" snapped the witch.

The blonde lady was bored because it was Monday morning and she'd eaten and drunk too much at the weekend, so she polished her nails and said, "We don't bother with animal accommodation much. If you own a lot of rabbits and you need somewhere bigger to live you'll have to make a lot of money."

"Thank you," said the witch. And she went home.

"What are you going to do now?" asked Simon.

"What she said – make a lot of money," said the witch.

And she got out her wand and made a hundred thousand pounds, all in new notes.

"I'm sure she didn't mean that!" stammered Simon, shocked.

"Come along," said the witch, and dragged Simon back down the High Street to the house agents.

"Got it," she said, slamming down her hundred thousand pounds on the shiny counter.

"Oh my gosh!" gasped the fat blonde, putting away her nail polish in an awful hurry. "I expect you'll want a manor house for that!"

"In a manner of speaking," said the witch.

The blonde lady curtsied and brought out a photograph of Monopoly Manor, a splendid house, with a garden the size of Buckingham Palace.

"It will do," said the witch, and picked up the keys.

Now it so happened that Monopoly Manor was right next door to the house in which Lady Fox-Custard lived. Lady Fox-Custard's house was also very grand. It had croquet lawns, fish ponds, stables for horses, and two enormous gate posts with stone lions sitting on the top of them.

When Lady Fox-Custard saw the witch going into the house next door she shouted, "Hey you, my good woman – you're in the wrong place. That house is up for sale."

"Was," said the witch. "I've just bought it." And she went inside.

Lady Fox-Custard was aghast. She suddenly recognized her shabby new neighbour as the witch who had once ruined one of her famous garden fêtes. She flew to the phone to complain to the mayor.

"She's got to be got out!" she shrieked.

"Nothing I can do about it, Felicity m'dear," apologized the Mayor. "Her money is as good as anyone's."

"But she's an old witch!" screeched Lady Fox-Custard.

The mayor wanted to say that so were a lot of other ladies of his acquaintance. But instead he just mumbled something and shot off to polish his gold chain.

"Vicar!" boomed Lady Fox-Custard, feverishly dialling the vicarage. "There's a dreadful witch of a woman moved in next door to me!"

"Now then, Flissy, dear heart. We must not be unkind, must we?" said the vicar. "Remember, we're all lovely people. You're lovely, I'm lovely, and I'm sure this dear old lady is lovely too." And he hurried off to check that his church hadn't had any more windows smashed in by vandals.

Meanwhile, Simon and the witch and her cat, George, were having a most enjoyable time.

"I feel like a duchess!" whooped the witch, finding a diamond tiara someone had left behind in a cupboard.

George had found a four-poster bed for himself and was nibbling at one of the posts to see if he liked the taste. It was delicious, so he finished most of it and then fell asleep on the powder-blue, silk quilt.

The drawing room was huge, but very cold. And the witch felt they must have a fire at once.

"You'll have to ring up a coal man," said Simon.

"Too expensive," said the witch. "These old chairs will burn nicely."

"I think they're Louis the Sixteenth's!" gasped Simon, horrified.

"Were, you mean, don't you?" said the witch. "Not my fault if he left them behind."

And she soon had a crackling big fire blazing. "How I ever lived in that scooty, little house down town I shall never know," sighed the witch, reclining blissfully in a gold chair which wouldn't burn. "I tell you what, Simon old thing, we must have a house-warming party. Go home and collect some of your friends. Say tomorrow about three o'clock."

Simon's friends didn't believe it. For one thing, they had never really believed that the old woman he was so friendly with was a proper

witch. And they certainly didn't believe that she could have found enough money to buy Monopoly Manor, which had only recently belonged to General Grand-Slam. But it was such a "nothingish" part of the holiday, they agreed to come and have a look.

"It will be a good laugh I suppose," said Sally, who was now on Book Six.

Jimmy Watson had already broken his supersonic model of Concorde so was feeling fed up; and most of the other children in Simon's class were bored because it was nearly time to return to school and their mothers kept dragging them off to town for visits to the dentist and things, and making them tidy their bedrooms.

When Lady Fox-Custard looked out of her window next day, she saw a gang of small, untidy children rollicking up the drive of Monopoly Manor. They were making slush snowballs and stuffing them down the hoods of each others' duffle coats.

"Ugh!" she shuddered. "How absolutely lootly dreadful!"

"Wipe your feet!" yelled the witch. "You're not at home now!"

The children looked around in awe. Simon had evidently been telling the truth. The witch really did seem to own the manor. With great respect, they took off their wellingtons and left them in the outer hall.

"Tea!" announced the witch.

George had been trying his hand at making chocolate mice.

The witch had knocked up a pile of beetle and banana sandwiches, a fly flan, and some tarantula trifle. As the children did not know what recipes the witch had used, they ate up the food hungrily, whilst Simon, who knew the witch's cooking habits of old, nibbled gingerly at a chocolate mouse and pretended that he'd just had an enormous lunch.

The witch wanted to show the children round her enormous garden, not because she was worried about them getting a spot of fresh air, but because she wanted to boast some more. But Sally decided it was too slushy out of doors, and what Sally decided, the rest of the class agreed with. The witch didn't like Sally much and gave her a burnt potato crisp.

"Oh look!" cried Jimmy Watson. "There's an old Eskimo woman looking through your window!" Jimmy Watson had only seen Lady Fox-Custard in flowery dresses at garden fêtes so he didn't recognize her now, in her polar bear coat and weasel fur hat.

"Hah!" croaked the witch. "That's a custard

tart heavily disguised as a skunk!''

"Lady Fox-Custard," explained Simon.

"She's spying on us!" hissed the witch. "She's as jealous as anything about my new manor."

She cocked her tiara at a wicked angle and whooped, "Let's give her something to be jealous about. We're all going to have a terribly posh party!" And she rang up André Prevo, who was a famous conductor she knew well, and asked him to come round and beat time to the record player. She was careful to hide the actual record player behind a large pillar, hoping that Lady Fox-Custard might think she had an orchestra there. The conductor, who loved parties, came at once.

"André Prevo!" gasped Lady Fox-Custard who absolutely adored culture. "How on earth did that old ragamuffin get *him*!"

"Give us a tune, André!" yelled the witch. "We want to play musical chairs."

Even Sally enjoyed this game, as André Prevo beat time to The Campbells Are Coming and Chop-sticks.

"How disgraceful!" gasped Lady Fox-Custard, glued to the window by an icicle. "I shall cancel my subscription to the Music Society!"

The witch drew the velvet curtains with a swish, but was careful to leave a chink wide enough for her new neighbour to spy through.

"Now let's play gambling games," said the witch very loudly. "Ludo for a hundred pounds a game."

"But I've only got seven pence for my bus fare," complained Jimmy Watson, alarmed.

"Ssssh!" hissed the witch, slapping her hand over Jimmy's mouth. "Pretend! Pretend! Pretend your parents have just won a million billion pounds on the pools."

"Oh!" giggled Jimmy, vastly amused. "I bet

five hundred pounds I win this game!"

"Scandalous!" groaned Lady Fox-Custard. "Little children gambling, and with all that money. And to think I told that wretched boy to get his dirty feet out of my lily pond. If only I'd known he was so rich and important!" And she went off home, very upset about the whole afternoon.

As soon as Lady Fox-Custard had removed herself and there was no one to show off to, the witch grew bored and tesky. "Get these wretched kids out of here," she snapped at Simon. "This is not a bingo hall!"

Jimmy Watson was quite shocked at the witch's sudden change of mood, but not so Sally, who knew the witch's spitefulness of old. She stumped off haughtily to fetch her wellingtons and deliberately forgot to say, "Thank you for having me, I've had a lovely time."

When the last of the children had left, Simon said, "That was a bit rude."

The witch yawned vastly and snapped both eyes shut, indicating that the visit was over. George smirked meanly at Simon and then gobbled up a pair of indoor shoes one of the children had left behind.

The Witch's Safari Park

The new term started, and Simon and his friends had a new teacher. Mr Bodley, the headmaster, came into Assembly and said that they were going to do lots and lots of exciting things during the term, and go places. Although he didn't exactly say what or where.

"He's wearing a new suit," whispered Sally.

"I know," hissed Jimmy Watson. "He got it from Oxfam for sixty pence. My dad was going to buy it only the lining was gone in the pockets."

"Where are we going, Sir?" asked Sally.

"That, my dear girl, is still to be decided; depending largely on how you behave."

And he whisked off his glasses with a flourish and put them in his pocket, whereupon they dropped straight through on to the floor.

Meanwhile, the witch was doing a great deal of flourishing of her own. She had put away her ridiculous, unfashionable, pointed hat into a plastic bag, and went round everywhere in her new tiara. All the time, she kept her eye on her next-door neighbour, Lady Fox-Custard. Noticing that Lady Fox-Custard had stone lions sitting on the top of her gate posts, the witch ordered a sculptor to carve two large elephants for her own posts.

"Don't you think they look awfully vulgar?" Lady Fox-Custard asked the vicar.

The vicar, who couldn't see why elephants should be more vulgar than lions, said he wasn't sure.

Lady Fox-Custard grew crosser and crosser. She spent half her savings building turrets on the top of her roof, and flew a large Union Jack from the bedroom window.

"That's lovely!" said the witch, popping her big nose through the laurel hedge. "I had tea with the queen the other day and I told her how hard you were trying."

"I wish you lived back in your nice little house," said Simon one day.

"Don't be silly," snapped the witch. "It wasn't a suitable place for a witch as extraordinary as I am." And she went off to town to queue for her free bus pass.

30

Next to the witch in the queue was an old man called Grandpa Gumption. "I think it's just marvellous!" he croaked.

"What is?" asked the witch, haughtily.

"Being able to go everywhere for nothing."

"Down the road and back again, I suppose you mean."

"Oh no!" said Grandpa Gumption, "I'm going to the Duke of Haughty-Culture's Safari Park. He's got a castle full of wild animals. I've brought sandwiches and everyfink."

The witch was suddenly enormously interested. "Mind if I come with you?" she asked.

"Please yourself Mrs," said Grandpa Gumption. "Be a spot of company for me."

Grandpa Gumption and the witch jumped on to an eighty-seven bus and beetled off in high spirits to the Duke's stately home.

The witch was quite astonished. There were some lions loafing around under the sycamores; giraffes delicately eating the tops of the trees; rhinoceroses thundering up and down the lawns, and chimpanzees jumping up and down on the tops of the cars and pinching aerials, windscreen wipers and anything else they could pull off. They even snatched Grandpa Gumption's chutney sandwiches. The witch was glad she'd tied elastic on her tiara. Nevertheless, she was *ab-*

solutely fascinated. She noticed that the Duke of Haughty-Culture was making a great deal of money. She also noticed that he seemed to be very high up and important. Grandpa Gumption took off his hat and bowed to the Duke every time he passed him, muttering "your dukedumb," and silly things like that.

It so happened that the witch had a sister who lived in Africa. Her name was Tombola. Her humble home was surrounded by wild animals. She had wild animals in her garden, on the roof, in her kitchen, under the bed. They were just a normal, everyday part of her life. She thought nothing of it.

Back at Monopoly Manor, the witch wrote to her sister.

"Dear Tommy,
I want you to do me a small favour.
Send me fifty assorted lions and tigers,
two giraffes,
a rhinoceros,
an armadillo,
and a couple of dozen chimpanzees.
I'll send you a coloured television and some new black stockings."

Tombola, who had been needing a new pair of black stockings for ages, collected the animals her

sister had asked for and dispatched them immediately.

George sniffed at them in disgust and went back to bed in a huff.

The witch typed out an advert and put it in the paper.

MONOPOLY SAFARI PARK
VERY WILD ANIMALS AND TEA AND BISKUTS
CHILDREN DUBBLE PRICE
25 PENCE

"It's a fiddle!" exclaimed Sally next day, when Mr Bodley had announced it at Assembly. "My mother certainly won't pay double price."

"It's history tomorrow afternoon," reminded Jimmy Watson.

That decided it. Next morning every child arrived with the required fifty pence for Monopoly Safari Park.

They squeezed and squashed on to the school bus, and wondered and wondered what on earth the witch had in store for them.

"Bet she's just got her old cat in a cage," said Sally.

"Or a few old rats she's found down by the lake," said Jimmy, who loved rats because he was so frightened of them.

But as they approached Monopoly Manor they could hear the most dreadful roars.

"Sounds louder than rats!" quaked Jimmy Watson.

The witch had been looking forward all day to the arrival of the school bus. She had dressed herself up in riding breeches, wellingtons, a safari helmet (with her diamond tiara round the brim of it) and was sporting a rifle slung over one shoulder.

"Welcome, Headmaster!" she greeted, leaping on to the roof of the school bus and pointing her rifle into the rhododendron bushes.

A giraffe wandered up from the flower beds, put its nose gently through the open window of the bus, and delicately ate up Mr Bodley's hat.

"Sorry about that," apologized the witch. "It was a mistake to wear a green hat. I think he thought you were a sycamore tree."

Mr Bodley pretended not to mind.

Next came a rhino. It smelt the bus all over, smashed the front headlights with its tusk, didn't like the smell of the bulbs, and trotted away in disgust.

"There's lots more excitement to come!" promised the witch, reloading her rifle and flinging herself flat on her tummy.

A chimpanzee leaped on to the bonnet of the bus and snapped off the windscreen wiper.

"He's pinched me windscreen wiper!" complained the bus driver.

"Chimps usually do that," explained the witch. "What a good job the weather forecast is dry with sunny spells."

Things were not going too well. On the witch's day out with Grandpa Gumption, the lions and tigers had growled fiercely and leaped around dangerously.

"Don't give up heart," she told Mr Bodley, reloading her rifle for the umpteenth time and firing a couple of shots in the air. "Any minute now we are going to be under attack. Wild animals are going to devour us whole. Try to, I mean."

"My mother's expecting me back for tea," said Sally.

The witch didn't like Sally much, on account of Sally being nearly off reading books and on to library books, so she said, "Home for tea, if a lion doesn't gobble you up first!"

But Tombola's animals were bored. They were used to the warmth and excitement of the jungle. They did not like the witch's garden much. It was damp and dismal. Water kept dripping off the rhododendrons on to their backs and soaking them. There were no snakes to watch out for, no poisonous spiders to avoid. Just the odd frozen-looking beetle scuttling past and minding its own business. The witch obviously expected them to swallow the headmaster whole, but the biggest lion had already given the headmaster the eye-over and decided there wasn't enough meat on him to feed a sick cub. He wished, heartily, that the witch would stop cracking away at her gun. His wife was due to have babies and the witch's antics were giving her a headache. He moved his beloved further under the bushes and refused to twitch even a whisker.

George watched the lions in disgust. "Flea-bitten lot!" he thought to himself. "Couldn't chase a lame dog."

He was not in a very good mood. Yet again, his mistress had forgotten to feed him. He had enjoyed devouring the last post on his four poster bed, but the canopy had just collapsed on top of him and this did little to improve his temper. He was fed up with everything. Fed up with the draughty manor in which he kept getting lost. Fed up with the way the witch kept showing off. And thoroughly fed up with the chatter, chatter, chatter of the children. With a ferocious meow, he hurled himself out through the bedroom window.

"Here comes a black panther!" screamed Jimmy Watson, laughing in his terror.

"Grrrrrrr!" spat George through the driver's window.

"Lor' sakes!" said the driver. "Shut all the windows!"

"What the heck d'you think you're up to?" bellowed the witch at George.

George leaped on to the roof of the bus and chewed the end of the witch's rifle so that it wouldn't shoot any more. Then he hung upside down by his tail and made horrible faces at the children inside the bus.

"Oh gosh!" cried Jimmy Watson, "we'll never get out of here alive!"

"Don't be a ninny," snorted Sally. "It's only that moth-eaten cat, George. Drive on driver."

"Yes, drive on," said Mr Bodley, the Head – recovering at long last from the shock and feeling huffy that Sally had thought of saying it first.

George squeezed one paw through a top window and pulled Sally's ribbon off. He jumped on it until it was a soggy mess and then he sank his claws deep into one of the bus tyres.

Pisssss, it went, and the whole bus toppled sideways.

The witch rolled off the roof like a black pudding and her language made even the driver put his hands over his ears. The lions and tigers came prowling out of the rhododendrons and watched in mild amazement. They thought George was marvellous. So did George. He had another jump on Sally's soggy ribbon and then walked off with great dignity towards the manor.

"Well!" said the witch, proudly. "That's a very fine animal! I'm sure we all enjoyed that. Well worth the money, eh?"

"Wasn't," said Sally. "Your cat's quite mad."

"What about me bus?" groaned the driver.

"What about it?" asked the witch. "Looks to me as if you could do with a new one. Doesn't look very roadworthy to me."

Mr Bodley kept opening his mouth to say something important and shut it again.

"Come on," said Sally. "We'd better start walking. I think the show is over."

"I think we'll visit the Flower Show next term," trembled Mr Bodley.

"Not with ME you don't!" said the driver.

"We had a great day out," Simon told his mother.

"I'm glad," said his mother. "I think these educational trips are just marvellous."

Pink Rock

Simon felt quite cross with the witch. He felt she hadn't been very polite to his friends so he decided not to go and see her for a while. The witch knew Simon was cross with her. She also knew that it wouldn't be very long before he came peeping through her hedge to see what she was doing, so she decided not to be in when he did. She would go on holiday. Lady Fox-Custard had just gone off on a winter holiday so it must be the right sort of thing to do.

She packed her nightdress, her toothbrush, her magic wand, and George into a suitcase and set off towards the station. She warned George not to meow until they got on to the train as she didn't want to pay for him.

"One," she said, at the ticket office.

"One what?" asked the ticket man.

"Ticket of course," snapped the witch. "You don't sell cabbages as well do you?"

"Where to?" drawled the ticket man.

The witch thought the ticket man was being very awkward so she grabbed him by the tie and hissed, "I am going on holiday. As you seem to be so very smart, you tell me where."

"Potato picking?" said the ticket man.

"Is that a *holiday*?" The witch was a little taken aback.

"Some people seem to think so," said the ticket man. "However, they don't do it in the winter. You could go skiing."

The witch gave him a withering look.

"Or you could go to the old folk's rest home and . . . rest."

The witch's stare became even colder.

"But most people go to the seaside for their holidays." And he gave the witch a ticket to Southend and told her to hurry along.

The seaside was wet and windy, but a row of monster hotels, the colour of seagulls, ran along the front. The witch eyed them carefully and chose the grandest. At once, a porter in uniform descended upon her and tried to take her suitcase.

"Thief!" yelled the witch, hitting him smartly.

"I was only trying to carry it for her," the startled porter explained to the manager.

"Rubbish!" snorted the witch. "That's his story."

The manager stared at the witch's shabby black dress with the soup stains blotching down the front of it, and then at her magnificent diamond tiara and couldn't decide whether to say, "Get out," or to bow. In the end he said, "Dinner will be served at seven."

The witch went up to her room and unpacked. Reasonably excited to be on holiday, she flung open the window expecting to see the sea and saw a small back yard stacked with milk crates.

Complaint number one, she wrote in her diary. *Must tell manager to change name of hotel from "Sea View" to "Milk crate View."* Then she swept up George and sailed down to dinner.

When the manager saw George he exclaimed, "Sorry, no pets allowed. Awfully sorry."

George leaped swiftly on to the back of the witch's neck and lay there very still.

"What pet?" asked the witch.

"That cat on your shoulder."

"Cat?" the witch looked puzzled. "Do you mean my lovely new fur collar?"

The manager stared hard at George and George stared back at him, just as hard, his whiskers

twitching only ever so slightly, yet *dangerously*.

"Awfully sorry," said the manager. He sat the witch at a table by the window and handed her a menu. It was very dull: asparagus soup, cod, and roast beef with winter cabbage. The menu itself had a nice cardboardy smell and George, disguised for the time being as a fur collar, ate it up hungrily.

The waiter, who'd never seen a fur collar do that before, hastily handed her another and promised himself to give up the habit of stealing the left-over wine.

The dining room was full of old gentlemen and old ladies. In the far corner sat a very delicate-looking old lady called Aunty Birdie.

"Oh!" screamed Aunty Birdie suddenly, "I've got a beetle in my soup!"

The witch leaped across the dining room, scooped up the beetle with one swoosh and swallowed it.

"Ugh!!!" shuddered everyone.

But Aunty Birdie was terribly grateful and thought the witch was extremely brave. Next day, she showed the witch round the town. They sat in a shelter on the prom and pretended it was warm until an icy green wave slopped over the

railing and nearly drowned them.

"It's nice in the summer though," chirped Aunty Birdie, emptying sea out of her little boots.

"Remind me to come again!" snorted the witch.

"Oh dear!" warbled Aunty Birdie. "You're not enjoying your holiday."

"Not a lot," said the witch.

So Aunty Birdie led her friend to an indoor place where there were fruit machines, and bumpy cars, but best of all, the witch thought, a huge stall of pink rock. At first, the witch thought the sticks of rock were pink wands until she tasted one, and then there was no stopping her. Every day, she dragged Aunty Birdie down to the rock stall. She had rock for breakfast, lunch, tea, and dinner. She crunched her way through rock walking sticks, rock lollipops, rock pigs, rock baskets of fruit, and rock dummies, until Aunty Birdie had to warn her that so much sticky rock couldn't possibly be good for anyone.

"Rubbish!" mumbled the witch, halfway through a pink and yellow walking stick. And then ... "Ow!!!"

"Oh! What's the matter?" twittered Aunty Birdie. "Have you got tummy ache?"

"Not my tummy. Ouch! It's my tooooooooooth!"

Aunty Birdie, who kept her own teeth in her handbag for safety, could only dimly remember what real toothache was like, but realized she must get her dear friend to a dentist at once. She hailed a ninety-nine bus which stopped right outside Mr Yankit, the dentist.

Mr Yankit had had a tiring day. His surgery had been nearly empty during the Christmas holiday, then as soon as the new term had started, children had come piling in on him in all directions. Now, this peculiar-looking old woman was staggering through his door, yelling blue murder.

"Name please?" sighed Mr Yankit.

"Witch," said the witch.

"A right one we've got here!" said the dentist to his receptionist. "Date of birth?"

"Eighteen hundred, and something and something," said the witch.

"Address?" continued Mr Yankit.

"Is this a quiz game?" snapped the witch, "Because if it is, how many eyelashes has an elephant?"

"Now look!" exploded Mr Yankit, winding the witch down flat in his dentist's chair. "Do you or do you not want me to pull your tooth out?"

"*Pull my tooth out*!!!" The witch went berserk.

She tore round the surgery like a black tornado, knocking instruments and half-finished sets of false teeth everywhere.

"Fetch me a hammer and chisel!" she yelled to Aunty Birdie.

"That's not right!" squealed Mr Yankit.

"And a crowbar," bellowed the witch.

"I need an anaesthetic," whimpered Mr Yankit.

"Don't know nothing about anaesthetics," roared the witch. "Are they pink?"

"Help me!" moaned the dentist.

"Shall I ring for the police?" asked his receptionist.

"No," said Auntie Birdie. "Leave this to me."

Bored with being an old lady, and spending all her winter months in grand hotels by cold seashores, she had recently taken up judo at evening class. She flew at the witch and caught her in a side four quarter hold.

"Now," said Aunty Birdie, "you are going into a deep sleeeeep."

"No, I aren't," yawned the witch.

"Oh yes, you are," said Aunty Birdie, "very deeeeep. And Mr Yankit is going to take that nasty old tooth out."

"No, he ain't!" screeched the witch, falling asleep with a sudden flop.

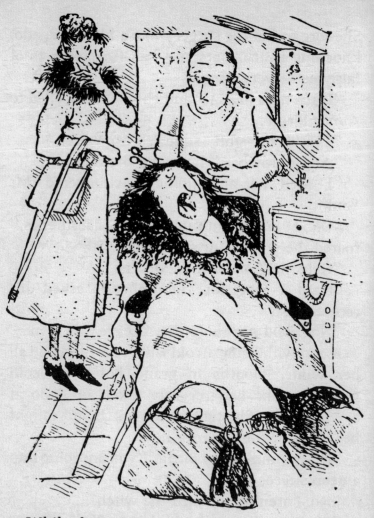

While the going was good, Mr Yankit yanked out the witch's tooth, wrapped it in a piece of gauze, and handed it to her when she woke up.

"If you put this under your pillow, someone might give you six pence for it," he said.

"Eeeeeh!" said the witch, pleased, and not remembering at all how badly she had behaved. "I must go home at once."

She shook hands with Aunty Birdie until Aunty Birdie's hand nearly fell off, collected her belongings from the hotel, and leaped on to the train.

It was lovely to be going home. Lovely to *be* home. There was the grumpy old ticket man, just locking up and putting on his hat. She gave him a stick of pink rock and hoped he'd get toothache. And there was Simon. He was looking for caterpillars along the railway sidings, or so he said.

"I've got a tooth," grinned the witch.

"I can see them," said Simon.

"No, silly, in my suitcase." She showed Simon. "I must dash home and put it under my pillow."

"You'll get six pence," Simon shouted after her.

"I know," chortled the witch, happily. It had turned out to be an exciting winter holiday. She vanished into a cloud of road dust.

Magically she was back at the station again.

"There *aren't* any caterpillars in winter," she told Simon. "You were just waiting to see me, weren't you?"

"No I wasn't," lied Simon, turning very red.

Angelica

Simon played at Monopoly Manor a lot after the witch returned, and his mother worried about him. She thought the old lady, (never, never would she believe she was a witch), was a little too old for Simon. Then suddenly, some new people arrived in the road. They were a Mr and Mrs Fortune and their small daughter, Angelica.

Simon's mother was delighted. Mr and Mrs Fortune looked highly respectable, and their dear little girl really did look like an angel. She wore spotless white all the time, and her fair ringlets curled daintily round her rosy cheeks; "Like candy floss or something," thought Simon.

"You're Simon, aren't you?" she asked, popping a button nose over the garden fence.

Simon was struck dumb. Angelica's eyes shone

like two cornflowers in a blonde hayfield. He tried to think of something clever to say and couldn't. Angelica opened the gate and came into his garden. His mother, who was looking out of the window, was pleased.

"I think my mummy is going to ask you to tea," whispered Angelica. "I'd like you to come. I have no one to play with."

"I'll come," said Simon, making a brilliantly long speech.

"I knewed you'd say that!" said Angelica, trotting off down the road bouncing her ringlets cutely.

Simon washed his face, and put on a new shirt, and arrived at the Fortunes' house a whole minute too early.

"Do come in, Simon," greeted Angelica. She was wearing a different white dress. "Mummy's got games and games and games for us! I expect we'll have lots of fun together."

Simon hung his cap in the cloakroom and waded across the carpet.

The Fortunes' house was like a small palace. The leather chairs shone, the plastic roses shone, the lumps of coal in the electric fire shone, even Mr Fortune's bald head shone.

"Shall we play Ludo?" asked Angelica.

"Yes," said Simon.

Angelica won every game. She kept shouting, "Six", when it was only a four or a one and Simon didn't like to tell her she was cheating.

"It's been lovely," she said. "You will come again won't you, Simon?"

"Yes," said Simon.

He walked home in a dream. He had never seen such a fairy-like creature in his whole life.

The next morning, the witch whizzed up to his front door on a skateboard. At the same time, Angelica arrived wearing yet another dress and a new white ribbon, as crisp as an ice cube.

"You've been invited *again*!" she gasped. "My mummy and daddy think you are very nice. And suitable."

The witch stared at Simon's suit with interest.

"Had it cleaned or something have you?" she asked.

Simon pretended not to hear.

"Coming skateboarding?" the witch went on, doing a hand-stand and wheeling crazily down the path.

"Do you know that disgusting old woman?" asked Angelica.

"Yes," said Simon, "I mean, no. I mean I used to," he stammered.

"Well, are you going with her, or are you coming home with me?"

The witch was still sailing expertly down the path and showing a great deal of grey knicker and black stocking tops, but grinning triumphantly, whilst Angelica's blue eyes shone even more brightly and innocently.

"I'm coming with you," said Simon to Angelica.

The witch zoomed straight over the garden gate, performing a double somersault as she flew, and shot off in a cloud of dust.

"What an absolutely dreadful, dreadful woman!" shuddered Angelica. "My daddy knows the mayor very, very well and he's going to get him to ban all skateboards."

"Yes," said Simon, looking wistfully after the witch.

For the rest of the afternoon he played Monopoly with Angelica, and spent most of his time in jail and not passing GO. Angelica bought hotels in Mayfair and Park Lane and kept fining him huge sums of money until he was broke and at last it was time for tea.

Angelica changed into yet another dress and Simon was forced to wash his hands and face so thoroughly, he felt it would have been quicker to have had a bath. The tea, when it arrived, was very small; just one scone each and a piece of sponge cake. This, as it turned out, was just as well as Mrs Fortune fired questions at Simon all the time. Could he do long division? Did he know how many wives Henry the Eighth had? Why did a Manx cat have no tail? Mr Fortune passed him the jam and asked him to spell "rhododendron". Angelica could do long division of money, find Katmandu on the map, say, "This is the pen of my aunt," in French, and spell rhododendron backwards.

Suddenly, Simon grew very sick of Angelica. He stared at her white dress and her cornflower-blue eyes and her flouncy candy floss hair, and he decided she was like a very chatty, sugary meringue. He longed to know what the witch was doing and how far she'd got on her skateboard. Halfway up the M1 at least, he thought.

"You'll come again terribly soon won't you?" Angelica was saying.

"Yes," said Simon, escaping down the Fortunes' drive and into the road. It was raining very hard and Simon made sure he was very muddy by the time he arrived home. Getting very wet and very muddy made him feel clean again, in an odd sort of way.

"Our turn to invite Angelica this time," said his mother, pleased Simon had a young friend.

"I'd like to dig up the garden," Simon said.

But his mother was already on the phone to Mrs Fortune.

Angelica arrived next day in a dress so white Simon was nearly blinded. He got out the Snap cards.

"There's a cat on your windowsill," Angelica remarked.

"We haven't got a cat," said Simon.

"Well there are two yellow eyes looking in at us." Simon looked up with interest. Slowly, the window began to open, and then a long hooked nose poked its way through the space, followed by a hollow chuckle.

"Oh!" cried Angelica. "It's that horrid woman you said you didn't know!"

"Snap!" said the horrid woman Simon didn't know, and vanished.

"Let's go after her!" shrieked Angelica, her blue eyes glinting like two pools covered in thin ice.

There were still skateboard skid marks on the path, made by the skateboard, and Angelica followed them enthusiastically.

"What are we going to do?" Simon asked, panting along.

"Capture her, of course, for trespassing and being a general menace to the public."

"Oh," said Simon.

The skid marks led straight through a ditch and Angelica emerged on the other side with her white dress black, and sopping wet.

"Gosh!" said Simon.

"My daddy, who knows the mayor very very well, will have her thrown into prison."

"But she hasn't *done* anything!" gasped Simon.

"That's all you know, silly boy!" said Angelica, dashing into the supermarket.

The skateboard tracks led straight up to a mountain of baked beans and Angelica dived in from the bottom. Baked beans tins rolled everywhere and Simon recalled a picture in his

Geography book of logging time in Canada.

The manager appeared and took Angelica's address and phone number.

"You'll pay for this, you little vandal!" he boomed.

"That's all right," sniffed Angelica, haughtily. "My daddy will settle up with you later. Please get out of my way."

A cackle came from amongst the frozen chips, and then again from outside in the darkness. Angelica pursued it through the Fire Exit Only door. It was inky black in the goods delivery yard and beginning to sleet again.

"When I catch that atrocious beggar woman,"

puffed Angelica, "and I tell my daddy, who knows the mayor so well, I daresay – and I do daresay, she'll probably be beheaded!"

"Actually," said Simon whose legs were beginning to ache with running," I should have told you sooner, I suppose, but she's a friend of mine."

"Oh don't be silly," said Angelica. "This is serious. Aren't you interested in Law and Order?"

"I think we're doing it next term," puffed Simon, thinking that perhaps it was a lesson he hadn't done yet.

Angelica gave him a scornful look and ran faster than ever. They ran so fast they found themselves past the street lamps and out in the country. The hedges were full of quiet squeaks and the trees full of hooting owls. Sleet flew in front of the moon and it was very cold and silent.

"Whoooo!" said a voice from somewhere.

There was a rattling noise, rather like the sound of a skateboard, and a black, lumpy shape darted in front of them and vanished. A thin cat with rather mad-looking green eyes scuttered past and also vanished. There was a long silence.

"Eeeeeh!" squealed Angelica. "I don't like it. I'm frightened. I want to go home."

So did Simon. He knew that the black, lumpy

shape was the witch fooling about, and that the thin cat with the mad green eyes was probably her cat, George, but he was cold and fed up. The witch certainly knew how to be annoying, but sometimes he could get quite annoyed himself. He was probably missing something great on TV. A girl with cornflower-blue eyes and blonde hair wasn't worth *that*.

He took Angelica's hand and floundered through the mushy undergrowth. The long grass stung his legs like so many frozen whips.

"Can't we find a bus stop?" whined Angelica.

"Can't we find Saint Paul's Cathedral?" snapped Simon.

Suddenly, the ground was hard beneath their feet and they were on a road. A huge lorry zoomed up and passed them.

"Was that a bus?" whimpered Angelica.

"I don't think so," said Simon. "It said Milk Marketing Board on the side of it."

A smaller light was now bobbing up the road.

"Maybe it's a bike," said Angelica.

"I don't think so," said Simon. "It's bobbing too much."

It was the witch.

She was carrying a small torch. Under one arm she was hugging a skateboard, and under the other, a large shabby handbag. Behind her loped a disenchanted, soaked black cat, its eyes madder than usual with unutterable boredom. (It too was sulking about missing television.)

"Hullo," greeted the witch. "Out walking?"

"Oh, yes," said Simon.

"We're waiting for a bus," sniffed Angelica.

"There aren't any," announced the witch. "I travel by skateboard myself."

"Those things are very dangerous," said Angelica.

"Fast though," chortled the witch, flying off at great speed and coming back again, "and convenient when there aren't any buses."

Angelica began to cry noisily.

"Your friend seems upset," remarked the witch. "And she's getting her lovely black dress all wet."

"It's white!" wailed Angelica.

The witch rummaged in her handbag and put on her glasses in order to scrutinize Angelica's dress.

"I don't think so," she said at length. "I'm not very good at colours. But if it's not black, then it's a peculiar sort of greyish-brownish, sort of midnight-bluish, sort of muddish colour," said the witch.

Angelica wailed more loudly than ever.

Another set of headlights came zig-zagging up

the road. The glare lit up the sleet which was now turning into fast snow. The witch stuck out a black leg and stopped the car. It was a Rolls Royce.

Sitting in the back of the car was a fat man smoking a cigar. It was the mayor. He had been to a hunt ball with Lady Fox-Custard and looked red and jolly. He recognized the witch immediately and wanted to know why she was so far from Monopoly Manor in such inclement weather.

"Been rescuing people," explained the witch.

"Ah, noble woman!" exclaimed the mayor. "What a work of charity!"

"One should be as charitable as one possibly can," observed the witch, piously, slinging George into the back seat, and shoving Simon and Angelica in after him.

"Allow me the pleasure of escorting you back to your residence," said the mayor, jolly with sherry.

"All right," said the witch.

Angelica explained that her father was Mr Fortune of number ten Laburnum Grove and that he wanted skateboards banned.

"Oh really," said the mayor. "Most interesting, most interesting. I must meet him some time."

Next day, the phone rang and Simon's mother hurried to answer it.

"What a shame!" she said.

"What is it?" asked Simon.

"Angelica has a dreadful cold. She won't be able to play with you today."

"Oh," said Simon.

The window slid up half an inch and a huge nose slid through.

"Coming skateboarding?" asked the witch.

"Yes please!" said Simon.

The Wonderful Cabbage Pie Party

The snow melted and the floods came. The primroses and the bluebells followed and Simon felt glad he was Simon, and seven. Angelica never came to play with him again and he was glad about that too. He was so glad about everything, he thought he might burst with gladness. And then Monopoly Manor caught fire and burnt to the ground.

There were firemen and hosepipes everywhere and a dreadful sickening smell which hung around in the air for miles. Some said it was the mayor who had dropped his cigar butt down the side of a chair. Others said that Lady Fox-Custard had done it on purpose. And yet others said that the witch's cat had been experimenting with gunpowder and home-made bombs.

Letters of sympathy plopped through the witch's letter box and George collected them with his sooty paws and took them up to the witch's bedroom. Actually, there was no upstairs anymore; the witch's bed had collapsed in a charred mess into the basement but she still talked about going "up" to bed.

George, his fur looking blacker and more dismal than usual, went around looking sorrowful, even though he had burnt down Monopoly Manor himself with a single match.

"D'you know what?" the witch said one morning. "This place is uninhabitable. It's back to the house agents."

George stared solemnly into the gloom and whisked a speck of soot off the witch's toast with his tail.

Simon arrived just as the witch was putting on her hat. (The tiara had melted in the fire, proving that the diamonds in it had not been real after all.)

"Lock the door," she told George, unnecessarily.

The blonde lady in the house agents seemed in a very disrespectful mood. She yawned so vastly Simon wondered how her head didn't split and fall off.

"We have a small residence down the road," she said. "S'been on our books for months. Can't get rid of it at all. Haunted or something silly."

The witch swept up the keys in the grand manner and strutted off. The house was indeed small. It stood six inches off the main road. Traffic rattled past it, deafeningly. Overgrown cabbages and nasturtiums quarrelled with each other across the small front garden, and chip papers and empty coke tins were strewn willy nilly amongst the weeds and up on to the front doorstep.

The witch's eyes grew dim and moist.

"It's mine!" she cried.

"So it is!" said Simon. "Your old house."

"Wipe your feet!" said the witch, turning the key in the lock, and failing to notice that George had his paws over his whiskers to hide a cunning smile.

Everything was just as she'd left it – dusty and incredibly untidy. A pile of unwashed pans stood in the sink. Above the cooker winked the star she'd once collected from the sky during a power cut. The television was on BBC2 playing test card music. Furniture George had only half eaten lay strewn across the floor, and mice were nesting, undisturbed, in the upholstery.

"Isn't it lovely?" gasped the witch.

Simon had to agree.

"Shall we have a party?" whooped the witch.

"It'd be great!" said Simon.

They made a cup of tea and sat down to write the invitations. They wrote invitations to the mayor, Lady Fox-Custard, Mr Bodley the headmaster, Sally, Jimmy Watson, and the whole class. And even to Mr and Mrs Fortune and Angelica. The witch licked envelopes until she was giddy and they just caught the five o'clock post.

"We've forgotten the vicar!" cried Simon.

"Drat!" said the witch, and she leaped on to her skateboard and flew off down the road after the red Royal Mail van.

The postman was sitting in his van, minding his own business and waiting for the lights to change, when a couple of eyes leered in at him through his side window. He nearly dropped dead, straight over his driving wheel, with the unexpectedness of it. He'd had mad motorists knocking his driving mirrors off, police bikes chasing him, and silly children on bikes wobbling past him on the wrong side, but he'd never been stopped by a pair of evil-looking green eyes.

"Are you going past the vicar's?" asked the witch.

"Could do," stammered the postman.

"Well, I hadn't time to write, but would you tell him to come to my party?"

"Will do," said the postman, zooming off like an express as the lights changed to green, and forgetting to ask where the vicar lived.

"All fixed!" the witch told Simon. "Now what are we going to give them to eat?"

They searched the fridge. There had been yet another power cut whilst they had been away and the food inside was not very nice. Not even George fancied it.

"Must have gone off," said the witch, whisking round with an air freshener and a fly killer.

"So what have we left for refreshments?" choked Simon.

The witch peered out into her garden.

"Oh no!" groaned Simon.

"Yes," said the witch. "Nasturtium sandwiches with pepper, properly prepared, are delicious."

Simon had to admit they didn't look too bad. At least they were different. Then the witch hurled herself with enormous energy into the flour bin and made two dozen cabbage pies with WITCHES RULE, O.K. written on the top of them.

They pushed the chairs to the side of the room, rolled back the carpet, and put on a record. Then they sat down and waited for the invited guests to arrive. But they didn't. George changed the record and absentmindedly ate one of the chairs.

"Wretched animal! Sabotaging the seating arrangements!" screamed the witch, catching him with a blow on the ear.

"Are you sure you put this address on the invitations?" asked Simon at last when the front door bell still went on not ringing.

"Of course I did!" snapped the witch. "I know

exactly what's happened. That snobby custard tart has gone and put everyone off. She always was dead jealous of me."

This was, unfortunately, true.

Finding out where the witch now lived, Lady Fox-Custard had leaped into her ancient car and chugged around the town telling everyone that the witch, who had thought herself so very grand, had moved to another house. A small, not very important sort of house. "Not a terribly nice end of town, especially after dark," Lady Fox-Custard told everyone, pretending to look worried but secretly bursting with glee. "It's sad really," she added. "But I don't suppose it could be much of a party. Poor old lady."

The mayor couldn't see himself getting a sherry at such an address and remembered that he had a new swimming pool to open.

The vicar was in the middle of writing a very tricky part of his sermon – vandals had smashed his biggest stained glass window and he needed money.

Sally and the rest of the class had a great pile of number work to do. Mr Bodley had promised himself an early night so that he would have the strength the next day to shout at the children for getting their homework all wrong.

Simon began to feel uncomfortable. The witch

had gone to a lot of trouble and nobody was turning up. It was so *mean*. All of a sudden the door bell rang.

"That'll be them!" shrieked the witch.

A collection of muttering dark shapes stood huddled on the doorstep. Green eyes blinked in the darkness right down the pavement.

"Hi!" said Hatty the Howl.

"Lovely to see you," said Winnie from Wapping.

"Your garden needs a bit of attention doesn't it?" said Gertie.

"My *relations*!" cried the witch, emotionally.

"Happy April Fools' Day," said Hatty the Howl.

"We just happened to be passing," explained Winnie from Wapping, "and we thought you might be having a party, for April Human Fools' Day."

"I am! I am!" roared the witch with laughter. "How clever of you all to guess. Everything's ready."

The witches trooped in one by one. There were fifty of them at least and their cats filled the back kitchen. George was hard put to know what to feed them on. He borrowed the witch's wand whilst she was busy cackling, and wondered if he could make it work. A lorry marked North Sea Foods rolled up to the back door and unloaded a ton of herring in the yard. The witches' cats stared at George with enormous respect and admiration.

Meanwhile, the witches had dumped their broomsticks in the cloakroom and were beginning to play party games. They played not very musical chairs, hunt the slipper, and postman's knock. Their shrieks disturbed the whole town. Constable Scuff arrived in his little blue and white panda car.

"There have been complaints," he coughed.

"What about?" yelled the witch.

"About the noise," shouted Constable Scuff.

"About whose nose?"

"The *noise!*" bellowed the constable.

"You're shouting," accused the witch.

"What's the yelling about?" Hatty the Howl wanted to know.

"I don't know, I can't hear him," said the witch.

Winnie from Wapping was knock knocking on the sitting room door and she came in and kissed Constable Scuff on the top of his helmet. "Ooooh! isn't he lovely!" she cried.

Constable Scuff didn't know what to do next. He took out his little book of police rules and looked up W for witches and K for kisses. But all he could find was W for wages snatch and K for killing, and neither of these seemed to fit the present circumstances.

"Don't look so worried," howled Hatty. "Have a little drink."

The constable did and immediately his worries got very small and muddled.

"Time for the cabbage pies," said the witch, and everyone sat down to eat.

"It's just lovely to have a man at our party," sighed Winnie from Wapping, now deeply in love with Constable Scuff. "But just as a matter of interest, why did you come?"

"Lady Fox-Custard sent me," mumbled the constable.

"Any relation to Lady Wolf-Pink-Blanc-mange?" giggled Gertie.

"Oh witty!" cackled the witch, but then grew serious in the middle of a mouthful of nasturtium sandwich and explained the whole story about the party. "She's just a jealous old tart and I'm sure she went round telling everyone my little house wasn't good enough."

"Not *good* enough?" hooted Hatty. "It's a darling, darling little place. Who does this silly fox think she is?"

"A lady," said the witch.

"We're *all* ladies!" exclaimed the witches, indignantly.

"He isn't!" sighed Winnie from Wapping, wrapping her arms tightly round Constable Scuff's neck.

"We'll have to do something about this Lady Snooty Custard," decided Gertie.

"It's against the law," choked the constable.

"What is!?" snapped Gertie. "We haven't even said yet what we're going to do. Maybe we're going to take her a lovely bunch of flowers."

The constable was now so muddled with the witch's home-made drinks and cabbage pie he couldn't think clearly what he ought to be saying next, so they borrowed his panda car and drove

off in a furious black flurry. Simon was both worried and excited. The witches drove like fury, and as they were in a police car, nobody stopped them.

They arrived at the gates of Lady Fox-Custard's residence.

"Is this it!?" gasped Gertie. "It's like a mausoleum!"

"What's a mausoleum?" asked Simon.

"Look it up in the dictionary, like I had to!" snapped Gertie.

They wandered round the grounds first, and Hatty, who was thirsty after the salty cabbage pie, drank up the fish pond, apologizing profusely to the goldfish. They arrived at the house and peered through the windows. There were suits of armour, luckily with no one inside them, swords and shields, and stags' heads on the walls.

"Heads without bodies," muttered Winnie, darkly.

There were sideboards crammed with china and silver ornaments, glass lilies under glass domes, pictures of cross-looking whiskery gentlemen, and a staircase so wide, one could have driven a ten-ton truck up it without hitting the bannisters.

"D'you think you have to pay to go in?" whispered Winnie.

The witch gave her a scornful look and pushed open a pantry window. The fifty witches flopped through it and started to wander around, giggling like naughty schoolgirls in their black uniforms.

"Isn't this a lark?" howled Hatty.

They came at last to a grand drawing-room. They peeped through the keyhole and saw, huddled round a one-bar electric fire, the mayor, the vicar, an old lady with a face like a crumpled sultana, and Lady Fox-Custard. They were playing a card game called bridge, which is a difficult game for grown-ups, and nothing at all to do with bridges.

"One no trump," the vicar was saying.

"Four clubs," said Lady Fox-Custard.

"Clubs!" exclaimed Winnie. "Do you think they're going to have a battle?"

"Might do," said the witch, knowingly. "It's quite a fierce sort of game."

"What a horrid cold place this is!" shivered Hatty. "Not nearly as cosy as your darling little house. And to think they came here instead of to your party."

"Let's shrink the place into a rabbit hutch!" suggested Winnie.

The witch smiled at Winnie for her helpful remark, but didn't think even her magic was quite strong enough to do that. But she wondered what she *could* do to teach Fox-Custard a lesson. It happened to be her turn to peep through the keyhole, but Awful Aggie, who had awful manners, pushed her out of the way and by mistake the drawing room door fell open and all the witches collapsed through it and arrived in a pile on the carpet.

"Good heavens!" gasped the vicar, who had never seen so many black stockings in one eyeful.

"An invasion!" shouted the mayor.

"Oh! No!" groaned Lady Fox-Custard, who recognized the witch on the top of the pile. "Get out! Go away!"

"Aaaah," said the aged lady with the face like a crumpled sultana. "Poor dear things. Don't send them away. Look how damp and shivery they are, and they're so *old*. Tell them to come in."

Lady Fox-Custard was seething with rage. But the Crumpled Sultana had once shaken hands with the Queen and Lady Fox-Custard did not want to lose her as a friend, so she said through gritted teeth, "Come in."

"Thank you, we is in," said Winnie. "How do you all do."

The gentlemen made space by the fire, and Hatty poked it which did little to improve it, as it was electric.

The witches made themselves enormously at home and taught the vicar how to play poker.

"Awfully jolly!" he kept saying, as he lost six weeks' Sunday collections.

The mayor lost his chain. But when Awful Aggie had bitten it and found out it wasn't real gold, he was given it back.

Then Hatty noticed the food, which was on the trolley.

"Catch!" she hooted, tossing sandwiches at everyone, and aiming a lump of salmon at Lady Fox-Custard.

"Oh dear! Oh dear!" The Crumpled Sultana lady wept with laughter until her hanky was just a little screwed up ball of wet lace. "What a time we're having!"

Lady Fox-Custard agreed with her: she had never had such a dreadful time. Horrid black feet jumped all over her cushions. Precious ornaments went over like skittles. Her dear little dog had scuttled off under the bookcase and got itself stuck. And her best carpet looked like a football pitch after a cup final.

"Oh!" exclaimed Aggie, suddenly. "The refreshments are finished."

"So they are," said everyone, dismally.

"What a jolly shame," sighed the vicar.

"Never mind," said the witch. "I've plenty more at home."

"Good gracious! Look at the time!" said the mayor. "I'd almost forgotten we were on our way to your party."

"I didn't actually forget, I was just ..." mumbled the vicar, dashing off to fetch his hat.

Lady Fox-Custard who had fainted flat into a cushion said nothing, so the Crumpled Sultana joyfully went in her place.

There were still plenty of cabbage pies and nasturtium sandwiches left in the witch's house. And George and his friends had eaten most of the furniture in the witchs' absence, there was plenty of room for everyone to squash in.

"D'you know m'dear," said the mayor. "I do like this little house so much better than Monopoly Manor. It's so much cosier."

"Yes, awfully jolly," agreed the vicar.

There was no one of any importance to complain to Constable Scuff about the din which followed, as everyone of any importance was already *at* the witch's wonderful cabbage pie party busy making the din.

"It's a really terrific party!" said Simon to the witch.

"Yes, but I just wish Fox-Custard could have come," lied the witch. "Odd the way she fell asleep so suddenly, but not to worry!"